Dear Parent:
Your child's love of reading starts here!

Every child learns to read in a different way and at his or her own speed. Some go back and forth between reading levels and read favorite books again and again. Others read through each level in order. You can help your young reader improve and become more confident by encouraging his or her own interests and abilities. From books your child reads with you to the first books he or she reads alone, there are I Can Read Books for every stage of reading:

SHARED READING
Basic language, word repetition, and whimsical illustrations, ideal for sharing with your emergent reader

BEGINNING READING
Short sentences, familiar words, and simple concepts for children eager to read on their own

READING WITH HELP
Engaging stories, longer sentences, and language play for developing readers

READING ALONE
Complex plots, challenging vocabulary, and high-interest topics for the independent reader

ADVANCED READING
Short paragraphs, chapters, and exciting themes for the perfect bridge to chapter books

I Can Read Books have introduced children to the joy of reading since 1957. Featuring award-winning authors and illustrators and a fabulous cast of beloved characters, I Can Read Books set the standard for beginning readers.

A lifetime of discovery begins with the magical words "I Can Read!"

Visit www.icanread.com for information
on enriching your child's reading experience.

I Can Read!

SHARED My First READING

Pete the Cat
Treasury

by Kimberly & James Dean

I Can Read Book® is a trademark of HarperCollins Publishers.

Pete the Cat Treasury

Pete the Cat: Pete at the Beach
Pete the Cat: Play Ball!
Pete the Cat: Too Cool for School
Pete the Cat: A Pet for Pete
Pete the Cat: Pete's Big Lunch
Pete the Cat and the Bad Banana

ISBN: 978-0-06-241797-8

March 2016

16 17 18 19 SCP 10 9 8 7 6 5 4 3 2

table of contents

Pete at the Beach

By James Dean

It is a hot day!

Pete the cat goes to the beach

with his mom and his brother, Bob.

"Let's go in the water,"
Bob says.
"Maybe later," says Pete.

Bob likes to surf.

He rides the big waves.

It looks like fun.

"I'm hot," says Pete.

"Go in the water," says Mom.

"Maybe later," says Pete.

Pete makes a sand castle.

His mom helps him dig.

Here comes a big wave.

And there goes Pete.

Oh, no!

Where did his sand castle go?

Bob rides a big wave.

"Wow!" says Pete.

"That looks like fun."

Pete and his mom take a walk.

They find seashells.

They see a crab.

Pete's feet get wet.

His feet feel cool.

The rest of him is hot.

It is time for lunch.

Pete eats a sandwich.

He drinks lemonade.

The sun is very hot.

And Pete is very, very hot.

Bob is wet and cool.

"Let's play ball," says Pete.

"No, thanks," says Bob.

"I want to surf."

Pete throws the ball.

His mom catches it.

"Let's get our feet wet,"
says Mom.
"Well, okay," says Pete.

The water is cool.

It feels good.

Pete goes in deeper.

Bob waves to Pete.
"I want to show you
how to surf!" he yells.

Pete does not say
"Maybe later."
He says, "Let's do it!"

"Lie on the board," says Bob.

Pete lies on the board.

"Paddle," says Bob.

Pete paddles out.

He waits for a big wave.

A big wave is coming!

"Stand up!" says Bob.

Pete stands up.

Then Pete falls down.

It was scary,

but it did not hurt.

"Try again later," says Bob.

Pete wants to try again now.

Pete lies down again.

He paddles out and waits.

Here comes a wave!

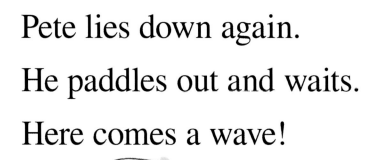

Pete stands up.

This time he rides the wave!

"Good job," says Bob.

Pete wants to surf all day.

Bob does, too.

So they take turns.

Pete and Bob rock and roll
with the waves.
What a great day!

It is okay to be afraid.

But it is more fun to surf!

Pete the Cat

PLAY BALL!

by James Dean

Here comes Pete the Cat.

Pete has a mitt.

He has a bat and a ball.

What will Pete do today?

Pete will play baseball!

Today is the big game.

The Rocks are playing the Rolls.

Pete and his team get set.

They play catch.

They take turns hitting.

It is time to play ball!

The Rocks bat first.
Pete waits for his turn.

Crack! The batter hits the ball.

He runs to first base.

"Way to go!" Pete cheers.

"Batter up!" says the umpire.

Pete goes up to bat.

The pitcher throws the ball.

Pete swings the bat.

He misses the ball.

Strike one!

The pitcher pitches again.

Pete swings too high.

Strike two!

The pitcher winds up.

He throws.

Pete strikes out.

But Pete is not sad.

He did his best.

Pete's friend Ben is up.

Ben hits a home run!

"Way to go!" cheers Pete.

The Rolls go up to bat.

The Rocks go to the field.

Crack! Here comes a fly ball!
"I've got it!" calls Pete.

The ball hits his mitt.

But Pete drops it.
He is not sad.
He did his best.

Another hit!
This time Pete catches it,
but he throws it too far.

Pete is up at bat again.

He wants to hit the ball.

The first pitch is too low.

Pete does not swing.

Ball one!

The next pitch is too high.

Pete does not swing.

Ball two!

The third pitch is inside.

The fourth pitch is outside.

Pete gets four balls.

Pete wanted to get a hit.

But a walk is cool, too.

The next batter gets a hit.

Pete runs as fast as he can.

Pete wants to score,

but he is out at home plate.

Pete is not sad.

He did his best.

The game is over.

The Rocks win six to three!

"Way to go!" calls Pete.

"Good game," the Rocks say.

"Good game," the Rolls say.

Pete did his best.

He had fun.

What a great game!

Pete the Cat

TOO COOL FOR SCHOOL

by Kimberly and James Dean

70

Pete wants to look cool.

He asks everyone,

"What should I wear?"

"Wear your yellow shirt,"
his mom says.
"It is my favorite."

So Pete does.

"Wear your red shirt,"
Pete's friend Marty says.
"It is my favorite."

So Pete does.

"Wear your blue shirt,"
Pete's brother Bob says.
"It is my favorite."

So Pete does.

"Wear your long pants,"
Pete's teacher says.
"They are my favorite."

2+2=4

So Pete does.

"Wear the shorts with the fish,"
Pete's friend Callie says.
"They are my favorite."

So Pete does.

"Wear the polka-dot socks,"
the bus driver says.
"They are my favorite."

So Pete does.

"Wear the cowboy boots,"
Grumpy Toad says.
"They are my favorite."

So Pete does.

"Wear the tie with the stripes,"
Emma says.

"It is my favorite."

So Pete does.

"Wear your baseball hat,"
his coach says.
"It is my favorite."

So Pete does.

Pete puts on all the clothes.

Does he look cool?

No.

Pete looks silly.

He also feels very hot!

Pete goes home.

He changes his clothes.

Pete puts on HIS favorite shirt.

Pete puts on HIS favorite pants.

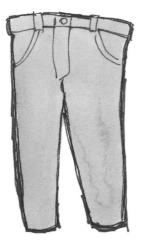

Pete puts on HIS favorite socks.

Pete puts on HIS favorite shoes.

Pete puts on his sunglasses.

Pete says, "Now I am COOL."

If you want to be cool,
just be you!

Pete the Cat

A PET FOR PETE

By James Dean

Pete is going to the pet store.

He is going to get a pet.

Pete wants a bird,

a hamster, or a lizard.

But then Pete sees a goldfish.

"That's what I want,"

he tells his mom.

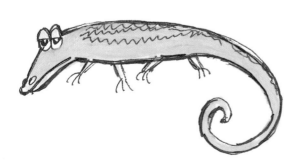

Pete's mom gets fish food.
"I'm going to call you Goldie,"
Pete says to his new pet.

"You are my first pet,"
Pete tells Goldie
on the way home.

Pete takes Goldie to his room.

He feeds her fish food.

"Now what?" asks Pete.

He can't play with Goldie.

He can't swim with her.

Pete knows what he can do!

Pete paints a picture of Goldie.

He paints four fins

and an orange tail.

"What a pretty painting,"
says Pete's mom.
"You can keep it," says Pete.

"Cool painting!" says Bob.
"Can you make one for me?"
"Sure," says Pete.

Pete paints a picture for Bob.

"Wow!" says Bob.

"It looks just like Goldie."

Bob shows Pete's painting
to his friend Tom.
Now Tom wants a painting, too.

Pete paints another picture
of Goldie to take to school
for show-and-tell.

"This is Goldie, my pet fish,"
Pete tells his class.

"I wish I had a picture
of Goldie," says Benny.
"I'll make you one," says Pete.

Everyone in Pete's class
wants a painting of Goldie!

Pete's grandma wants
a painting, too.

Pete has a lot to do.

He has to feed Goldie.

He has to do homework.

Pete paints and paints.
He makes paintings for
everyone on his list.

At last Pete is done!

He worked hard.

There is no paint left.

Pete's paintings are a big hit!

Pete is happy to be done.

But Pete is not done.
Now everyone in town
wants a painting of Goldie!

Pete gets more paint.
"I don't know what to do,"
he says to his mom.

"I wish I could paint
pictures for everyone.
I just don't have time."

Pete's mom has an idea!
She tells it to Pete.
"Great idea!" says Pete.

Pete gets right to it.

This time he works outside

and makes a huge painting.

Honk! Honk!
Beep! Beep!
Here comes Pete!
He has made one painting
of Goldie for everyone
in town to enjoy!

What a great day!
When Pete gets home, he tells
the real Goldie all about it.

Pete the Cat

PETE'S BIG LUNCH

by James Dean

Here comes Pete!

It is lunchtime.

Pete is ready to eat.

What should Pete eat?

A sandwich would be nice.

Yes, Pete wants a sandwich.

Pete opens the fridge.

He takes out a loaf of bread.

He finds a yummy fish.

He adds tomato and mayo.

Pete looks at his sandwich.

It is too small.

Something is missing.

Pete knows what it needs.

His sandwich needs an apple.

Pete loves apples!

His sandwich needs crackers.

Crackers are crunchy.

Pete loves crunchy crackers!

Pete looks at his sandwich again.
It is still too small.

Pete is very hungry.

Pete adds a pickle.

Pete adds cheese.

Pete adds an egg,

two hot dogs,

a banana,

and a can of beans.

Something is missing.

Pete adds ice cream!

He takes three huge scoops.

Pete's sandwich
is too big
for Pete to eat.

Pete wonders
what to do.
Pete thinks
and thinks.

"I've got it!" Pete says.
Pete calls all of his friends.

He asks them to come over.

Everyone goes to Pete's house.
They are all very hungry.

Pete shows them
his big lunch.

"Are you hungry?" asks Pete.
Pete's sandwich is big enough
for everyone.
"Dig in!" says Pete.

Pete's sandwich is good.

Pete's sandwich is VERY good.

Pete's sandwich is all gone.

Pete's friends are full.

They liked Pete's big lunch.

"Thanks for lunch,"
Pete's friends say.
"Thanks for sharing!"

"You're welcome," Pete says.
Sharing is cool.

Pete the Cat
AND THE
BAD
BANANA

By James Dean

Pete the Cat is eating
a banana.
Pete loves bananas.

They are sweet and tasty
and easy to peel.

Every morning, Pete puts
a banana in his cereal.

Sometimes Pete puts
a banana on his
peanut butter sandwich.

162

But one day,

Pete eats a bad banana.

The banana is gross.

The banana is mushy.

The banana is yucky.

Pete's tummy hurts.

"I will not eat bananas again,"

Pete tells his mom.

Pete's mom tries to help.
She bakes Pete's favorite:
banana bread.

Pete will not touch it.

She makes Pete
a banana cream pie.

Pete will not eat it.

She gets Pete

a big banana split.

"No thanks," Pete says.

Instead, Pete tries a lemon.

It is yellow like a banana.

Pete tastes it.

"Yuck!" says Pete.

The lemon is sour.

Pete tries a pickle.

It is long like a banana.

Pete tastes it.

"Better," Pete says,
"but not as good as a banana."

Pete tries an orange.
It has to be peeled
like a banana.

The orange is sweet,
but it is too juicy.
It makes Pete's paws sticky.

Pete tries fish, plums, rice,
hot dogs, watermelon,
and his mom's nut bread.

Pete eats them all!
He is not hungry
for bananas anymore.

Then comes the big race.
What should Pete have
for breakfast?

A pickle?

No, Pete doesn't eat pickles for breakfast!

A hot dog?

No, Pete just had a hot dog
for dinner last night.

A lemon?

No. That's just silly.

Pete wants a banana.

They're yummy and healthy.

Bananas are the best!

"Do you have another banana?"
Pete asks.

"Of course," says Greg the Monkey.

Pete peels the banana slowly.

It is not brown.

It is not mushy.

Pete takes a teeny, tiny bite.

It is a yummy banana.

It is the best banana ever!

Thanks to Greg and his banana,
Pete wins the race.
Pete is bananas for bananas!

If you want
to be cool,
just be you!

Pete the Cat